Serena
the Salsa
Fairy

For Saskia Rose Lewis
with lots of love.

Special thanks to Sue Mongredien

ISBN-10: 0-545-10622-2
ISBN-13: 978-0-545-10622-1

12 11 10 9 8 7 6 5 4   12 13/0

Printed in the U.S.A.   40

First Scholastic Printing, May 2009

Serena
the Salsa
Fairy

by Daisy Meadows

SCHOLASTIC INC.

New York   Toronto   London   Auckland
Sydney   Mexico City   New Delhi   Hong Kong

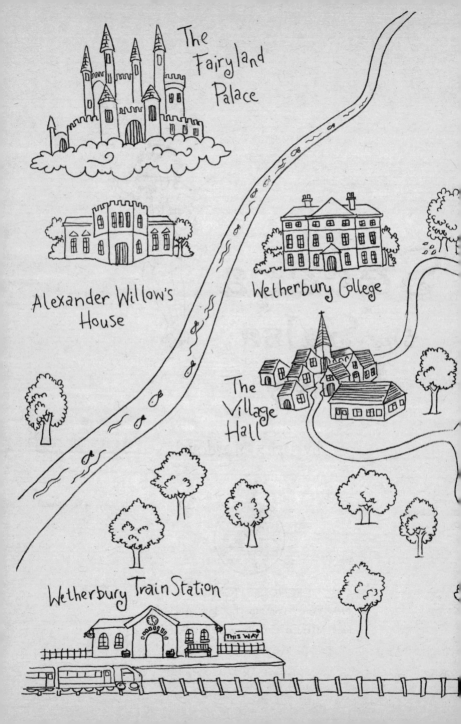

The Fairyland Palace

Alexander Willow's House

Wetherbury College

The Village Hall

Wetherbury Train Station

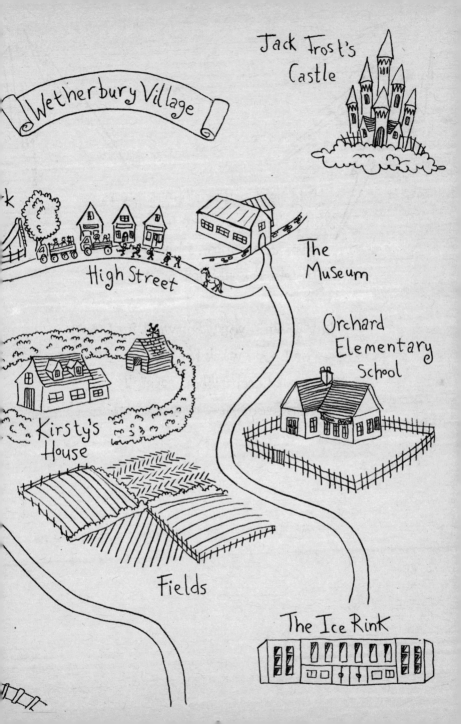

Hold tight to the ribbons, please.
You goblins may now feel a breeze.
I'm summoning a hurricane
To take the ribbons away again.

But, goblins, you'll be swept up too,
For I have work for you to do.
Guard each ribbon carefully,
By using your new power to freeze.

Contents

Fun at the Fiesta

"See you later, Mom," Kirsty Tate said, as she and her best friend, Rachel Walker, got ready to leave the house.

"Four o'clock, in front of the Village Hall," Mrs. Tate reminded the girls. "I should be done with my work by then. I'm sure you'll have a great time at the

fiesta. I can't wait to see all of the dancing and costumes. Promise me that you'll stick together — it's going to be very crowded."

"We will," Kirsty promised. Then, as the two friends headed down the road, she said to Rachel, "Of course we'll stick together. Isn't that when we have all our best adventures?"

Rachel grinned. "I hope we have another one today," she replied.

Rachel was staying with Kirsty's family for school break, and the girls were having a very exciting week. A *fairy* exciting week, in fact, because they were helping the Dance Fairies find their missing magical ribbons! The dance ribbons helped dancers perform their best throughout Fairyland as well as all around the human world. But Jack Frost had stolen the ribbons in order to make sure his goblins would dance well at his parties. When the fairy king and queen had heard about the stolen ribbons, they hurried to Jack Frost's ice castle to get them back.

Unfortunately, Jack Frost had seen them coming, and he had immediately cast a spell to send all the ribbons into the human world, with a goblin to guard each one. Since the ribbons had been missing, dancing had been going horribly wrong in Fairyland and all over the world. Luckily, Kirsty and Rachel had helped the fairies find the ballet, disco, rock 'n' roll, tap dance, and jazz ribbons. These ribbons were now safely back with their rightful fairy owners. There were still two dance ribbons out there somewhere, though, and the girls were anxious to track them down.

"The salsa ribbon is still missing," Kirsty said, as they walked toward the center of the village, where the fiesta was taking place. "I wonder if the goblin guarding it will be attracted to the salsa music and turn up at the fiesta today. I hope so!"

Rachel nodded. "If he's anything like the others, having the ribbon will just make him want to dance, dance, dance," she agreed. "And with all that salsa music playing, I bet he won't be able to resist it."

At first, the girls had been surprised to
see that the goblins who were guarding
the dance ribbons could dance really
well. In fact, dancing seemed to be the
only thing they wanted to do! Any time
they heard a tune in their particular
dance ribbon's style, they seemed drawn
to the music. The fairies had explained to
the girls that it was actually the ribbons'
magic that made the goblins dance so
well. The power of the dance ribbons

 was so strong that
they made anybody
nearby dance
wonderfully — even
clumsy goblins!
Kirsty glanced
around. "Well, I
hope the goblin with

the salsa ribbon does turn up," she said quietly. "That way, we might be able to get the ribbon away from him and safely back to Serena the Salsa Fairy," she added. "If we don't, the salsa dancing is going to be ruined today!"

At that moment, the girls turned the corner onto High Street. For a second, they completely forgot all about goblins as they took in the sight before them.

High Street looked

amazing. Colorful banners and streamers were strung up everywhere. Balloons bobbed on the lampposts, and the girls could see tents and booths lining the street, selling food and drinks. Music was playing, everyone was smiling, and there seemed to be a great buzz of excitement in the air.

"This is so cool!" Rachel said, her eyes shining as she gazed around.

Kirsty grabbed her hand. "Come on," she said eagerly. "Let's go over to the museum, where the parade is going to start. It might be fun to see everyone getting ready."

"OK," Rachel agreed. "And let's keep an eye out for a goblin!"

As they walked toward the museum, they came across a group of friends gathered around a papier-mâché piñata. The piñata was in the shape of a pineapple, and it was dangling from a tree branch. The kids were taking turns putting on a blindfold and whacking the piñata with a stick, hoping to crack it open and release the goodies inside.

"There's Lucy!" Kirsty said, spotting one of her school friends and waving. Lucy smiled and called them over. "Do you want to take a turn?" she asked. "Ooh, yes, please," Kirsty said at once, hurrying up to the piñata. Rachel followed and was given the blindfold to tie around her friend's eyes. Then Rachel and Lucy turned Kirsty around three times before putting the stick in her hand.

Dizzy, Kirsty stumbled toward where she thought the piñata was and bashed it with the stick as hard as she could. *Crack!* The pineapple split open and lots of candy, small toys, and glitter tumbled to the ground. Everyone cheered and crowded around to gather up the treats.

Rachel was just about to join them

when she suddenly noticed a tiny spark of light shoot out of the piñata and up into the air. She knew that it couldn't be a sparkly piece of glitter, because it was flying up and not down.

"That's strange!" Rachel said to herself. Then an exciting thought struck her — could it be a fairy?

The Parade Gets Underway

Rachel watched closely as the sparkle zipped over to the side of a small tent. She turned to tell Kirsty, but her friend was just pulling off the blindfold and talking to Lucy. Rachel was worried that she might lose sight of the sparkle, so she raced around the tent for a closer look. Her heart was thumping as she turned

the corner. Then she smiled. It was Serena the Salsa Fairy! She was perched on the edge of the tent roof, waving at Rachel. Rachel waved back with a grin, just as Kirsty came around the corner with a handful of candy.

"Do you want some?" Kirsty asked Rachel. "I picked up tons!"

Rachel was too excited to think about candy. "Look, Kirsty," she whispered, pointing up at the tent roof. "Serena's here!"

Serena fluttered down toward the girls, and Kirsty saw that she had long black hair, pinned back with a beautiful red

rose. The fairy
was wearing a
red top and a red
skirt with gorgeous
orange ruffles.

The girls had met
all the Dance Fairies on
the very first day of their adventure, so
they recognized Serena right away.

"Hello, Rachel. Hello, Kirsty," the
fairy said, smiling as she landed on
Kirsty's shoulder. "I'm here to find my
ribbon. I've got a strong feeling it's
somewhere nearby — and I have to get
it back so that all the dancing at the
fiesta goes well today!"

"We'll help look for it," Kirsty said at
once. "We've been keeping an eye out
for goblins, but we haven't seen any yet."

"There are going to be lots of salsa
dancers in the parade," Rachel added.
"The goblin might be attracted to the
salsa music and follow them."

Serena's face brightened. "Let's try to
find the goblin before the parade starts,"
she suggested. "Otherwise it will be
awful."

"What are we waiting for?" Rachel

said determinedly. "Let's get out there
and find that goblin!"

Serena hid herself behind Kirsty's hair
as the girls headed for the starting point
of the parade. They arrived to find
people rushing around, preparing for the
parade to begin. Dancers applied last-
minute touches of makeup. Helpers
smoothed costumes and checked hair

ribbons, while the sound crew tested the speakers and microphones.

"It's hard to spot a goblin when everyone's rushing around like this," Rachel said. "And there are so many people here. How are we ever going to find him?"

Serena was fidgeting on Kirsty's shoulder. "I don't know, but I hope we see him soon," she remarked. "The parade is going to begin any minute!"

The girls searched the crowds.

Leading the parade was a group of women in bright flamenco dresses with lots of ruffles and matching scarlet shoes.

The women were followed by gleaming white horses, wearing tall, white feathers set in golden headdresses.

"Wow!" Kirsty said, distracted by the sight. "They look amazing!"

Rachel was examining everyone in search of a tell-tale flash of goblin green. "The goblin definitely isn't around here," she said after a moment or two. "Not unless he's dressed as a horse!"

Just then, a voice came over the loudspeaker. "Welcome, everyone, to the Wetherbury Fiesta. Let the parade begin!"

Serena and the girls looked at each other in dismay. "We're too late," Rachel said. "It's starting!"

Salsa Slip-ups

Whistles sounded from the crowd, there was a thunderous drumroll from one of the marching bands, and then some lively salsa music started up. Despite their worries about the ribbon, Kirsty, Rachel, and Serena couldn't help feeling excited by the festive carnival mood.

"Let's stand here and watch," Rachel

suggested. "We might see the goblin going by in the parade."

Serena nodded. "I hope so!" she said. "We'll have to watch out for anyone who's dancing really well. It might be because the ribbon is close to them."

The flamenco dancers waved and blew kisses to the crowd. They led their horses down the street, shaking tambourines and swishing their skirts as they paraded along.

People were clapping and cheering as the horses trotted by, their white coats gleaming in the sunshine and their feathery headdresses fluttering in the wind. After them came the Scintillating Samba Band. The musicians played drums, trumpets, and maracas as they marched along in black pants and ruffled white shirts.

"This is wonderful!" Serena beamed, clapping along in time to the music.

"And so far everyone's just been walking, rather than dancing, so nothing's gone wrong."

"Ooh, look, she goes to my school!" Kirsty said excitedly, as a salsa dance class full of kids followed the samba band. She waved at a girl in a blue dress who was twirling around with a partner. "Oops," Kirsty said, as the girl saw Kirsty, waved back, and then bumped into her partner.

"Oh no," Rachel said with concern as she saw another girl from the dance class trip. "It looks like the dancing is beginning to fall apart."

Serena watched anxiously. "If only I had my ribbon." She sighed. "I could have stopped this from happening!"

Next came a group of salsa dancers, shimmying their way along the parade route. A woman in a long red evening dress danced at the front, carrying a sign that read "Cuban Break Salsa Group!" She was just waving it above her head and smiling at the crowd when, suddenly, she stumbled awkwardly on her high heels, dropped the sign, and almost fell over.

Serena winced. "We have to find my ribbon before someone gets hurt," she said. "Where is that goblin?"

"I don't know," Rachel replied, as one of the salsa dancers accidentally stepped on his partner's toe. "Ouch!" she exclaimed sympathetically.

The Cuban Break Salsa Group passed by, and a float came next. There were a lot of *oohs* and *ahhhs* from the crowd as it moved past, because the whole platform had been set up to look like an exotic garden paradise. Palm trees and some amazing painted scenery made the whole float bright with colorful flowers, birds, and butterflies. The salsa dancers on the float were wearing fantastic costumes to make themselves look like tropical birds, and they were performing some very complicated salsa dance moves. It wasn't long before the crowds lining the street were applauding and cheering louder than ever.

"Those salsa dancers are really good!" Serena said. "What's going on?"

Kirsty grinned. "I've got a feeling your

ribbon must be on that float with them,
Serena," she suggested.

"I bet you're right, Kirsty!" the little
fairy agreed.

"Let's follow the float," Rachel
suggested eagerly.

Kirsty glanced around as the float
moved past, and her face fell. "It's going
to be tricky," she said. "There are so
many people here! We're really going

to have to try hard to get through the crowds."

Serena smiled. "Why walk, when you can fly?" she asked cheerfully. "Let's find someplace quiet for me to work some fairy magic."

Kirsty and Rachel managed to squeeze their way through the crowd to an empty side street, and then Serena waved her wand over them. With a swirl of fiery orange sparkles, Kirsty and Rachel were transformed into tiny fairies.

Kirsty flapped her

delicate wings happily, admiring the way
that they shimmered in the afternoon
sunshine.

"Now we can get really close to
the float and get a better look at the
dancers," Rachel suggested, as the three
friends fluttered high above the crowd.

"Good idea," Serena agreed, "but we'll have to be very careful that no one spots us."

Quick as a flash, the three fairies zoomed down to the float and hid behind one of the palm trees. "Keep your eyes peeled for the goblin," Kirsty whispered, peeking out from behind a palm leaf. "He must be here somewhere, and the sooner we spot him, the better!"

Goblins Disguised

The three fairies gazed around at the dancers and studied them carefully, but it wasn't easy to make out their faces. The dancers were whirling around so fast, they seemed more like colorful blurs than real people.

"I can't believe they can dance so

quickly on a moving float!"
Kirsty marveled.

Serena nodded.
"It makes me
even more sure
that the salsa
ribbon must be
here, helping
them keep
their balance,"
she said.

Just then,
Rachel spotted
two shorter
dancers in the
middle of the float.
They were both dancing
exceptionally well. One was
dressed as a parrot and the other as

a bird of paradise with a spectacular, rainbow-colored feathery tail. Both dancers had wings attached to their arms, and beaks fastened over their noses with elastic. "Look!" Rachel hissed, pointing the short dancers out to Serena and Kirsty. "Those two are the best dancers of all."

The three fairies watched as the parrot took the bird of paradise's hand. The bird of paradise

spun around under the parrot's
outstretched wing.

"Nice," Serena said approvingly.
"That's called an Alemana Turn," she
told the girls. Then she stared closely
at the dancers. "They're very small,
aren't they?"

"Maybe they're goblins!" Kirsty
whispered.

The three fairies looked
at one another in
dismay. Two
goblins? One
was bad
enough, but
outwitting two
would certainly
be double trouble.
"At least only one of

them will have the freezing power," Kirsty said, trying to be positive, but she couldn't help shivering a little. Before sending the goblins into the human world to guard the Dance Fairies' ribbons, Jack Frost had given them each the power to freeze things. But the girls knew that the magic only lasted for as long as the goblin had a magic ribbon in his possession.

The three friends zoomed a little closer to the dancing goblins, hoping to spot Serena's orange ribbon. They zipped between dancers really quickly, so that they wouldn't be seen by

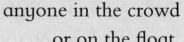

anyone in the crowd
or on the float.
Eventually, they
reached a palm
tree near where
the goblins were
dancing, and landed
on one of its big leaves
for a closer look.

Suddenly, Serena let out an excited
squeak and pointed at the bird of
paradise's feathery tail. There,
among his feathers, was
a long, fiery orange
ribbon. The salsa
ribbon!

"I'll get it," Kirsty
offered, and she made

a dive for the bird of paradise's tail. She was just about to grab the ribbon when the other goblin noticed her. With a yell of surprise, he yanked his friend toward him, hastily twirling the bird of paradise under his arm so that the feathery tail was out of Kirsty's reach.

The two goblins lifted up their beaks and made rude faces at Kirsty, Rachel, and Serena. Rachel gasped as she noticed the parrot goblin's very pointy nose. He was the same goblin who'd been guarding Jessica the Jazz Fairy's ribbon, which they'd only gotten back yesterday!

The pointy-nosed goblin glared at them. It was clear that he recognized the girls, too. "We'll have to get away from those pesky fairies," Rachel heard him warn his friend. "They're after your salsa ribbon!"

And then, before Kirsty, Rachel, or Serena could move, he'd grabbed the other goblin's hand. Together, they took a running jump off the float.

The three fairy friends could only watch as the goblins opened up their feathery arms and glided to the ground. Then they raced off through the crowd toward the nearby park.

"After them!" cried Rachel.

Goblins Give Themselves Away

As Kirsty zoomed after the goblins, she noticed that a few people in the crowd were staring after the running birds in confusion. Fortunately, another band began a salsa tune, so the people soon turned back to the parade. Meanwhile, Kirsty, Rachel, and Serena flew after the goblins as fast as they could. The three

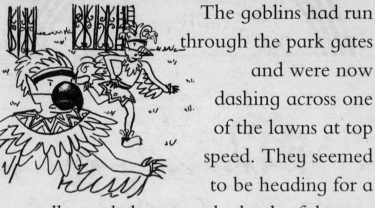

fairies made sure they all stayed high up in the air, so that they were out of sight.

The goblins had run through the park gates and were now dashing across one of the lawns at top speed. They seemed to be heading for a small wooded area at the back of the park. Kirsty, Rachel, and Serena could hear them yelling to each other in panicked voices.

"Where can we hide? Where should we go?" the parrot goblin shouted.

"Birds live in trees, don't they?" the goblin with the ribbon replied. "Let's hide in a tree — nobody will notice us there!"

The parrot goblin
seemed to think this
was a very good
idea, because he
began scrambling
up the nearest tree
trunk. The bird-of-
paradise goblin
climbed
awkwardly after
him, his colorful
tail dragging
through the autumn
leaves on the branches
as he went.

Moments later, Kirsty,
Rachel, and Serena arrived at the base of
the tree. Up through the gold, brown,
and orange leaves, they could see the

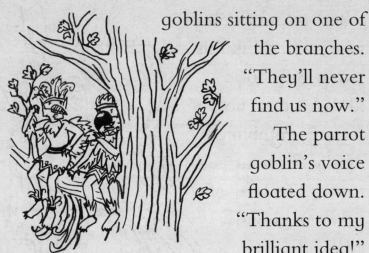

goblins sitting on one of the branches. "They'll never find us now." The parrot goblin's voice floated down. "Thanks to my brilliant idea!"

"We're masters of disguise!" the bird-of-paradise goblin happily agreed. "Invisible to the rest of the world!"

"I think I make a very good bird," the parrot goblin said. "Listen to this. *Cheep! Cheep!*"

Rachel watched as the bird-of-paradise goblin elbowed his friend. "Parrots don't cheep," he hissed. "They squawk and say funny things."

Kirsty saw the parrot goblin scratch his head. "Um, birdie wants a cracker!" he screeched. "Birdie wants a cracker!"

Rachel, Kirsty, and Serena all looked at one another and couldn't help giggling. The goblins weren't well-disguised at all.  Their bright costumes stood out against the autumn leaves, and they were much, much bigger than real birds.

"Nobody would be convinced by that parrot impression," Kirsty laughed.

"'Their disguises are awful!" Rachel giggled, and then a thought struck her. "You know, those goblins have given me an idea." She turned to Serena. "Serena, could you use your magic to camouflage me and Kirsty, so that we blend in with the leaves of the tree? If we're disguised, we might be able to sneak up on the goblins and grab the salsa ribbon!"

Serena nodded. "That's a great idea," she said, waving her wand over the girls. A stream of glittering orange sparkles

poured from the tip of her wand and fizzed around Rachel and Kirsty. As the mist of sparkles cleared, Rachel grinned to see that she and

Kirsty were now wearing wonderful outfits made from fall leaves. "Your hair's still dark, though," she said to Kirsty, noticing how it stood out against the deep yellow and orange colors of Kirsty's outfit. "I wonder . . ."

But Serena was already waving her wand again. Another swirl of magical sparkles surrounded the girls. Kirsty and Rachel gasped as they saw each other's skin and hair turn orange, too.

"Perfect!" Kirsty laughed. "Now, let's get that salsa ribbon!"

Salsa Success

Rachel and Kirsty fluttered silently up
the tree and perched on a branch just
below the goblins. The goblins were
getting carried away with their bird
noises, and it was all Kirsty could do not
to burst out laughing as she listened to
the terrible racket.

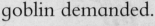

"*Tweet! Tweet! Tweet!*" twittered the bird-of-paradise goblin. "*La-la-la-la-la!*"

"What's that all about?" the parrot goblin demanded. "What's with the la-la-las?" The other goblin looked annoyed. "I'm a songbird, aren't I?" he replied. "That's just one of my songs!"

"What, la-la-la?" the parrot goblin asked, looking doubtful. "Real birds don't sing la-la-la!"

"I'm just getting in the mood," his friend said sulkily. "How about this? *Coo, coo, cooo!*"

"You're not a pigeon!" the parrot goblin snapped. "Look, you either do this properly or don't do it at all!"

Rachel didn't dare look at Kirsty as the goblins started a heated argument about bird noises. She knew she'd burst out laughing if she and Kirsty made eye contact! The goblins seemed to have forgotten all about keeping themselves hidden. Their voices were getting louder and louder as they argued.

Rachel edged quietly along the branch toward the bird-of-paradise goblin's tail. She pressed herself against a twig, waiting for the

right moment to strike. Then, as the two goblins began fighting about who had the best costume, she darted forward and quickly plucked the orange ribbon from the goblin's feathery tail.

Kirsty grabbed hold of it, too, and the two brave fairies flew away from the tree. They carried the ribbon between them. As the ribbon trailed through the air behind the girls, the parrot goblin let out a great squawk of shock.

"Look! Those leaves are flying off with our ribbon!" he cried in amazement.

His friend stared after them. "They're not leaves. They're pesky fairies! But they've turned orange!"

"Well, I'm not letting them get away with this!" the parrot goblin declared, making a frantic lunge for Kirsty and Rachel.

"Careful!" yelled the bird-of-paradise goblin as the parrot goblin bumped into him. And then both goblins lost their balance and tumbled out of the tree! Luckily, they landed on a big pile of autumn leaves.

The goblins jumped to their feet, looking furious, but Serena was pointing her wand at them as a warning.

"It's time for you two to go," she said firmly, "or I'll

turn *you* orange! And who ever heard of an orange goblin?" The parrot goblin pulled off his beak and threw it down grumpily. "This is your fault," he fumed to his friend. "If you hadn't been doing your la-la-las so loud, they never would have found us up there!"

"My fault!" the other goblin retorted. "What about you and your parrot screeches?" Rachel and Kirsty hovered in

the air and smiled at each
other as the goblins
stomped away
angrily, still
grumbling.
"Those
goblins won't
be causing any
more problems at
the fiesta, thank goodness!"
Rachel said happily.

"Here you go, Serena," Kirsty said as
they handed the salsa ribbon to her.

Serena waved her wand over the
ribbon, shrinking it to its Fairyland size.
She then reattached it to her wand with
a happy smile. The ribbon shone a deep,
warm orange in the sunshine, and fairy
sparkles glittered from one tip to the

other. "Thank you, girls," she said. "I'm so glad to have my ribbon back. Now all the salsa dancing will be as good as ever!"

She waved her wand at Kirsty and Rachel and turned them both back into girls, with their normal skin, hair, and clothes. "There," she said. "Now you're all ready to enjoy the rest of the fiesta."

"Thanks, Serena," Rachel said. "We will!"

The girls called good-bye to the little fairy as she zoomed away in a last flash of orange sparkles.

"It's almost time to meet Mom," Kirsty said, glancing at her watch. "But first I want to see what else is in the parade, and I feel like doing some dancing myself!"

She and Rachel made their way back to High Street, where the crowds were still clapping and cheering for the dancers in the parade.

The girls were glad to see that none of the dancers seemed to be having any

trouble now. They were all dancing wonderfully, and the audience was moving and clapping in time to the salsa music.

"Everyone's having a great time now," Rachel said, smiling as she joined in the dancing. "What a fabulous day!"

Kirsty nodded, twirling around on the spot. "And who knows? Tomorrow might be even better," she said excitedly. "After all, there's only one more magic ribbon left to find!"

THE DANCE FAIRIES

Serena the Salsa Fairy has
her magic ribbon back. Now Rachel
and Kirsty need to help

Isabelle
the Ice Dance
Fairy!

Help the girls find the final ribbon!

A Sparkling Skate

"I can't wait to see the show!" Kirsty Tate told her best friend, Rachel Walker, as Mrs. Tate dropped the girls off outside the ice rink. After her mom promised to pick them up when the show was over, Kirsty exclaimed, "Oh, I just love ice dancing!"

"So do I," Rachel agreed.

"Good afternoon, ladies and gentlemen!" A voice boomed over the loudspeakers as the girls walked inside. "Welcome to the Glacier Ice Rink. We have a wonderful show for you today, so get ready to see all of your favorite fairy tale characters dancing on ice! The show begins in twenty minutes."

There was a long line of people waiting to show their tickets, so the girls joined the line.

"I wish I could ice dance," Rachel said longingly. "I can skate pretty well, but I'd love to be able to do all those jumps and spins."

"Me too!" Kirsty laughed. "My friend Jenny's playing Sleeping Beauty in the show today, and she's an amazing ice dancer! Let's go to the dressing

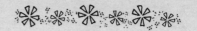

room and wish her luck before the show starts."

Rachel nodded but her expression was anxious. "With Isabelle the Ice Dance Fairy's ribbon still missing, isn't Jenny's dancing going to be in danger?"

Kirsty nodded sadly.

"I'm just hoping the goblin with Isabelle's ribbon turns up at the ice rink today," Kirsty whispered as they handed in their tickets. "After all, each ribbon is attracted to its own special type of dance."

Rachel nodded. "I hope the goblin's here somewhere," she replied. "Mom and Dad are coming to take me home tomorrow, so we have to find Isabelle's ribbon before then."

The girls went into the auditorium

where the ice rink was surrounded by rows of seats. Music was playing over the loudspeakers as people began to sit down.

"Let's go and see Jenny," said Kirsty, and she took Rachel over to the exit that led to the changing rooms.

As they entered the hallway, Rachel gave a gasp. She thought she'd just seen something green disappear around the corner at the end of the hall.

Could it have been a goblin? she wondered.

"What's the matter, Rachel?" Kirsty called, as her friend ran down the hallway.

Rachel stopped at the corner, looking this way and that, but there was no sign of goblins. "I thought I saw a goblin run around this corner!" she exclaimed, as

Kirsty joined her. "But there's no
one here."

"We've got goblins on the brain,"
Kirsty said, shaking her head.
"Remember what Queen Titania said —
we have to let the magic come to us!"

"Well, I hope it comes quickly,"
Rachel said with a sigh. "It would be
great if we could find the missing ribbon
before the show starts."

RAINBOW magic™

THE PETAL FAIRIES

Keep Fairyland in Bloom!

RAINBOW magic

These activities are magical!
Play dress-up, send friendship notes, and much more!

📖 SCHOLASTIC
www.scholastic.com
www.rainbowmagiconline.com

HiT entertainment

RMACTIV3

RAINBOW magic™ SPECIAL EDITION

Three Books in Each One—More Rainbow Magic Fun!

Joy the Summer Vacation Fairy
Holly the Christmas Fairy
Kylie the Carnival Fairy
Stella the Star Fairy
Shannon the Ocean Fairy
Trixie the Halloween Fairy
Gabriella the Snow Kingdom Fairy
Juliet the Valentine Fairy
Mia the Bridesmaid Fairy
Flora the Dress-Up Fairy
Paige the Christmas Play Fairy
Emma the Easter Fairy
Cara the Camp Fairy
Destiny the Rock Star Fairy
Belle the Birthday Fairy
Olympia the Games Fairy
Selena the Sleepover Fairy
Cheryl the Christmas Tree Fairy
Florence the Friendship Fairy
Lindsay the Luck Fairy

■SCHOLASTIC

scholastic.com
rainbowmagiconline.com

HIT entertain
RMSPECIA